JUN 1 2 2009

With thanks to Francis Firebrace and his people
for granting permission to retell these ancient
Aboriginal legends as stories for children – J.V.M.

To the spirit of Pauline E. McCleod,
a great storyteller and a beautiful sister – F.F.

Stories from the Billabong copyright © Frances Lincoln Limited 2008
Text copyright © Donald Payne 2008
Illustrations copyright © Francis Firebrace 2008

First published in Great Britain and the USA in 2008 by
Frances Lincoln Children's Books, 4 Torriano Mews,
Torriano Avenue, London NW5 2RZ
www.franceslincoln.com

British Library Cataloguing in Publication Data
available on request

ISBN: 978-1-84507-704-4

Illustrated with acrylics

Set in Berkeley

Printed in China

1 3 5 7 9 8 6 4 2

STORIES FROM THE
BILLABONG

Retold by James Vance Marshall
Illustrated by Francis Firebrace

F
FRANCES LINCOLN
CHILDREN'S BOOKS

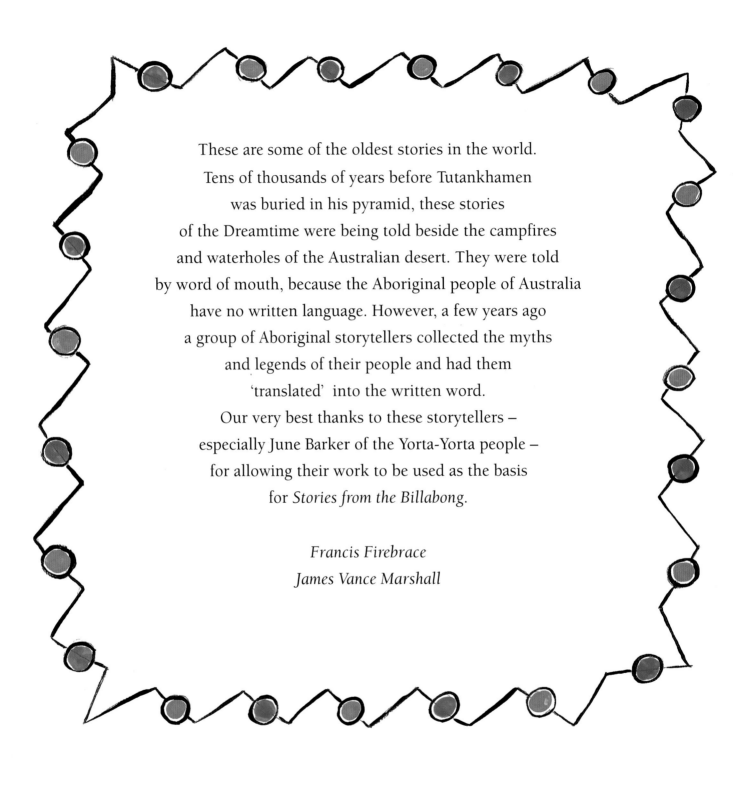

These are some of the oldest stories in the world.
Tens of thousands of years before Tutankhamen
was buried in his pyramid, these stories
of the Dreamtime were being told beside the campfires
and waterholes of the Australian desert. They were told
by word of mouth, because the Aboriginal people of Australia
have no written language. However, a few years ago
a group of Aboriginal storytellers collected the myths
and legends of their people and had them
'translated' into the written word.
Our very best thanks to these storytellers –
especially June Barker of the Yorta-Yorta people –
for allowing their work to be used as the basis
for *Stories from the Billabong*.

Francis Firebrace
James Vance Marshall

CONTENTS

The Rainbow Serpent and the Story of Creation

In the beginning, there was no life on the surface of the Earth. But beneath the surface the Great Mother Snake, the Rainbow Serpent, lay asleep.

She slept for a long, long time. Then one day she woke up, uncoiled herself, and crawled into the open. As she moved slowly over the flat, dry, empty land, she said to herself, "This isn't much of a place." So she used her magic to make rain.

It rained day after day. Week after week. Month after month. Year after year. And after a while the tracks left by the body of the Rainbow Serpent filled with water. This is how the long winding rivers, the billabongs and the waterholes came into being.

Sometimes, as the Rainbow Serpent moved forward, she pushed her nose into the Earth, and the soil piled up in front of her. This is how the mountains, the hills and the valleys came into being.

In some places, the milk from her breasts soaked into the Earth and made it fertile. And here great rainforests sprang up, and all sorts of grasses, and carpets of bright-coloured flowers.

When the Rainbow Serpent had made the land to her liking, she went back inside the Earth and woke the creatures who, like her, had been asleep there.

First she woke the mammals, and led them up to the best places for them to live. The dingoes, who didn't need much water, she took to the desert. The kangaroos, who liked grasses and leaves, she took to the bush. And the amphibious tree-frogs, who liked things cool, dark and wet, she took to the rainforest.

Then she woke the birds. The eagles, who could fly high and far, she took to the mountains. The galah, who could fly only a short distance, she took to the billabongs. And the emus, who couldn't fly at all, she took to the plains, where they could run about to their hearts' content.

Then she woke and brought out the creatures who lived in water. The barramundi she took to the rivers. The frogs she took to the shallow ponds. And the turtles she took to the lagoons.

Next she woke the insects: the ants, the beetles, the spiders and the scorpions. And she showed them the rocks, the crevices and the sandy places where it was best for them to live.

Last of all, she brought out a woman and a man. And she took them to a place where there was lots of food and water, and taught them the lore by which they should live.

What the Rainbow Serpent taught them was very simple. She told them they were to respect all living creatures. For the kangaroos and the galah and the barramundi were their cousins, children of the same creation. And she told them they were to respect and care for the Earth – for its rocks and trees and waterholes were sacred, since they too were part of the world she had created.

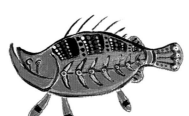

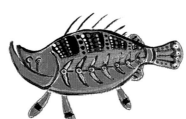

And before she went back to sleep, beneath the surface of the Earth, the Rainbow Serpent gave the woman and the man a warning. She reminded them that they were not the owners of the Earth. They were its guardians. And she told them that if, through greed or for pleasure, they abused the Earth instead of caring for it, then she might have to emerge again and create a new world. And in this new world, woman and man would have no place.

The Rainbow Serpent

Aboriginal Australians believe that our Earth was shaped by a number of mythical beings, among them the Rainbow Serpent. And they believe that these mythical beings actually became part of the Earth. So to Aboriginal people the world we live in is a sacred place, a gift from the gods to be loved and cared for. They are appalled at the way many people regard the Earth as something to be owned and exploited.

No one knows exactly how old the story of the Rainbow Serpent is. But we do know that the Aboriginal people came to Australia more than 60,000 years ago, crossing by a landbridge from Indonesia during the last Ice Age. And we know that the Aboriginal rock carvings, which include the Serpent, were made at least 40,000 years ago. So Aboriginal culture, isolated from the rest of the world, is by far the oldest continuing culture on Earth.

How the Kangaroo got her Pouch

Mother Kangaroo was finding her baby, young Joey, a real handful. Whenever her back was turned, he would go hopping away to explore. She was afraid that one day she would lose him.

One morning, when Joey and his mother were feeding in the plains, a weak and very old wombat came crawling towards them. "I am sick and blind," he said. "I am hungry and thirsty. And I haven't a friend in the world."

Mother Kangaroo felt sorry for him. "I'll be your friend," she said. "Hang on to my tail, and I'll take you to where there's water."

So off they went.

It wasn't an easy journey. The old wombat kept letting go of Mother Kangaroo's tail. And Joey kept getting left behind. But at last they came to a waterhole. And the old wombat drank and drank and drank.

Then he started complaining again. "Oh, I'm so hungry! I'm starving! I haven't eaten for days."

"Hang on to my tail," Mother Kangaroo said. "And I'll take you to where there's some nice grass."

So off they went again.

This time, the journey was even more difficult. The old wombat kept losing his grip on Mother Kangaroo's tail. And Joey was tired and cross and wanted his mother to carry him; but her little arms were too short. So they struggled on.

12

At last, they came to some lovely, lush grass. And the old wombat ate and ate and ate.

Mother Kangaroo watched him, happy that he seemed, at last, to be enjoying himself. Suddenly she froze. She stood very still and very straight. Her nose twitched. She sensed danger.

A moment later a hunter, carrying a boomerang, came running towards them. His eyes were on the wombat.

"Unless I help the poor old thing," Mother Kangaroo thought, "the hunter will kill him." She jumped up and down in front of the hunter, to attract his attention, then went bounding away across the plains.

The hunter told himself that kangaroo steak would be a lot tastier than stringy old wombat. So he ran after Mother Kangaroo. He flung his boomerang at her.

But Mother Kangaroo could run faster than the hunter. And she kept out of range of his boomerang. She led him on and on and on. Through the scrub. Across the plains. Over the hills, until at last the hunter was exhausted, and gave up, and went home disappointed.

Then Mother Kangaroo went hopping back to where she had left her Joey and the wombat.

They weren't there.

Mother Kangaroo was distraught. She rushed this way and that, looking for them. She looked into the scrub. Behind the boulders. And in the shade of the trees. She kept crying, "Joey! Joey! Where are you?" And at last she saw him, asleep under a gum tree.

She cradled him in her little arms. "Oh, Joey!" she whispered, "I thought I'd *really* lost you this time!"

She asked him what had happened to the old wombat. But all Joey could tell her was that he "sort of disappeared".

What neither Joey nor his mother knew was that the weak old wombat wasn't in fact a wombat at all. He was the Spirit of the Creator who had come down to Earth to find and reward the kindest and gentlest of all the animals.

The Spirit of the Creator decided that no animal could possibly be more kind and more gentle than Mother Kangaroo. So that night, while Mother Kangaroo slept, the Spirit left beside her a gift: a dilly bag… a shopping bag made of string.

When Mother Kangaroo woke and saw the dilly bag, she wasn't sure what to do with it. So she tied it round her waist. And in an instant, the Spirit turned it into a pouch.

So now young Joey had a place where he could rest, sleep, keep warm and hide. And Mother Kangaroo had a place where she could keep her Joey close beside her when he was little or in danger.

And ever since, kangaroos and their fellow marsupials have been the only animals in all the world that have pouches, in which they give birth to and look after their children.

Kangaroos

The animals living in Australia are different from the animals in other parts of the world. About 50 million years ago, the land mass of Australia became separated from all the other land masses (like Africa, Antarctica and South America). Australian animals were cut off from the rest of the world, and they evolved to suit their own particular environment. While most animals run using their four legs, kangaroos hop, using only their two back legs. And while most animals' babies are born fully formed and are separated from their mothers at birth, the babies of kangaroos are born blind, only partially formed, and no more than 2.5 cm (1 in) long. They spend their first 6-9 months in their mother's pouch.

There are more than 50 different species of kangaroo. Largest are the red kangaroos, well over 2m (7 ft) tall and weighing up to 90 kg (200 lb). Smallest are the mouse-kangaroos, only a few inches long, and weighing less than 28 gm (1 oz). Most species live in family groups of about ten or twelve, led by a dominant male. They are peaceful creatures, browsing on grasses and leaves. When frightened, the largest species can hop away at over 21 km (30 miles) an hour. But they are not often frightened. For in Australia there are only three predators that larger kangaroos need to be afraid of: dingoes (wild dogs), crocodiles and men.

Why Frogs can only Croak

Every morning, Lyrebird came down to the stream to sing. He had the most beautiful voice. He could imitate the sound of all the other birds: the boom of the cassowary, the cooing of the pigeon, the laugh of the kookaburra, and the beautiful song of the bell bird.

One day, while Lyrebird was singing, he noticed something unusual in the stream. The water was flowing fast, and there were lots of bubbles in it. Most of the bubbles were white. But one bubble looked dark. And there seemed to be something inside it.

As Lyrebird watched, the dark bubble burst. And out fell a little green frog.

Little Green Frog swam to one of the water-lilies. He climbed on to it, puffed out his chest, and stared this way and that.

Lyrebird had never seen such a strange-looking creature. "Hullo," he said, "I'm Lyrebird. Can you sing?"

The frog shook his head.

Lyrebird tried again. "Can you talk?"

The frog shook his head.

Lyrebird thought, "This isn't a very interesting creature." He was about to leave, when he heard the voice of the Spirit of the Creator.

"Lyrebird," the Spirit said. "this little frog is your brother. Teach him to sing."

Lyrebird knew the lore demanded all creatures should share whatever they had with one another. So he started to give the frog singing lessons.

Frog turned out to be a quick learner. Soon he could sing all the high notes. And all the low notes. He could even "throw" his voice, so it seemed as though it was coming from somewhere else.

Lyrebird was delighted. One day he said to him, "I do believe you can sing better than me." And he invited all the other animals to come and listen to the frog.

When the other animals arrived at the stream, and saw Little Green Frog, they were not impressed. But as soon as he started to sing, they were very impressed indeed. For he sang most beautifully. Not only did he imitate the sounds of other animals, he imitated the sounds of nature: the sound of waves breaking on the shore, the sound of wind in the leaves, and that most beautiful sound of all, the sound of rain falling on hard, dry land.

His audience were full of praise.

That night, when all the animals had gone home, the frog climbed on to his favourite lily-leaf. He puffed out his chest and shouted, "I can sing better than the lyrebird! I am the greatest singer in the world."

The other frogs told him not to be so conceited. But he kept on shouting, "I am the greatest! I am the greatest!"

The frog who was his girlfriend told him to be quiet. But he cried, "I am so great a singer, I could make the moon come tumbling out of the sky to listen to me!"

"Right," the girl frog said. "Go for it!"

The frog took a deep breath, and started to sing. He sang so beautifully, all the other frogs came out to listen. The waterfalls roared with delight. And the babooks screeched with excitement. But the moon took no notice at all.

Next night, the frog tried again. He sang louder, and longer, and even more beautifully. But still the moon took no notice.

The frog couldn't believe it. Next night, he tried again. He sang on and on and on. Louder and louder and louder. But the moon just kept sailing along among the clouds.

Suddenly, to the frog's horror, his voice gave out. He had strained his vocal cords to breaking point. He opened his mouth, but all that came out was a dismal croak.

And from that day to this, when the moon is bright, you will find frogs coming out of the water, and gathering together. But when they try to sing, all they can manage is *"Croak! Croak! Croak!"*

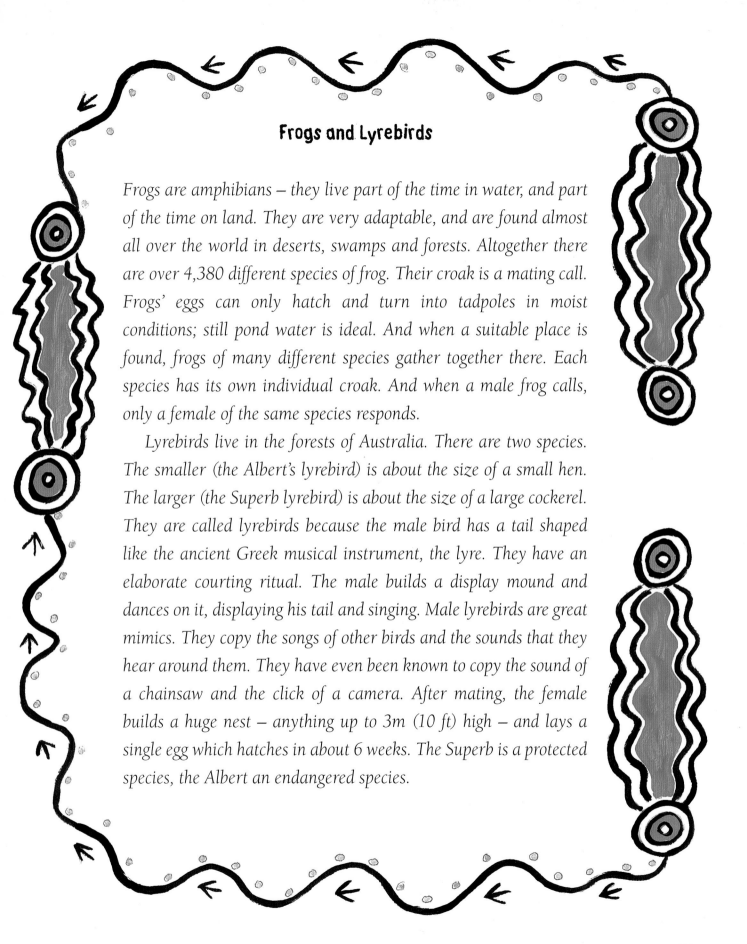

Frogs and Lyrebirds

Frogs are amphibians – they live part of the time in water, and part of the time on land. They are very adaptable, and are found almost all over the world in deserts, swamps and forests. Altogether there are over 4,380 different species of frog. Their croak is a mating call. Frogs' eggs can only hatch and turn into tadpoles in moist conditions; still pond water is ideal. And when a suitable place is found, frogs of many different species gather together there. Each species has its own individual croak. And when a male frog calls, only a female of the same species responds.

Lyrebirds live in the forests of Australia. There are two species. The smaller (the Albert's lyrebird) is about the size of a small hen. The larger (the Superb lyrebird) is about the size of a large cockerel. They are called lyrebirds because the male bird has a tail shaped like the ancient Greek musical instrument, the lyre. They have an elaborate courting ritual. The male builds a display mound and dances on it, displaying his tail and singing. Male lyrebirds are great mimics. They copy the songs of other birds and the sounds that they hear around them. They have even been known to copy the sound of a chainsaw and the click of a camera. After mating, the female builds a huge nest – anything up to 3m (10 ft) high – and lays a single egg which hatches in about 6 weeks. The Superb is a protected species, the Albert an endangered species.

Why Brolgas Dance

Long ago, on the banks of the Darling River, there lived a girl whose name was Brolga. Brolga loved to dance. But in those days, women and girls were not supposed to dance. They were supposed only to clap their hands and stamp their feet, while the men danced.

One evening, while the men were dancing, Brolga couldn't restrain herself any longer. She jumped up, and started dancing with the men.

At first, her tribe were shocked. But when they saw how beautifully Brolga danced, they agreed to let her continue.

Soon, Brolga became famous, and people came from all over the outback to watch her dance. A lot of men fell in love with her and wanted to marry her. But Brolga wasn't interested. "If I marry," she said, "I will have to cook and look after children. That's not for me. All I want to do is dance."

And because she danced so wonderfully, her tribe were happy to let her have her way… all her tribe, that is, except for an evil old magician called Broolie-Broolie. Broolie-Broolie wanted Brolga all to himself. He watched her every move.

Brolga's friends were worried by this. "When you dance," they told her, "stay close to our camp, so we can look after you, and see the evil old man doesn't harm you."

At first, Brolga was careful, and danced only around the place where her people were camped. But after a while she grew careless. And one day she went dancing across the plains, over the hills and into the desert, far, far away from her tribe.

The evil Broolie-Broolie watched her.

He used his magic to turn himself into a whirlwind. He went rushing after her. Swirling round and round, he picked her up. "Marry me, Brolga!" he shouted.

But Brolga said "No!"

"Marry me," Broolie-Broolie shouted again, "or I'll make sure you won't ever marry anyone."

"No," she cried. "Never!"

The wicked old man was furious. He used his magic on Brolga to change her into something altogether different. Then he dropped her in the middle of the desert.

When Brolga picked herself up, she looked at her feet, and, to her horror, saw she no longer had the feet of a girl. She had the feet of a bird.

She looked at her arms, and she saw she had the wings of a bird.

She felt her mouth, and knew she had the beak of a bird.

Poor Brolga wept. "Never again," she thought, "will I be able to dance."

However, when she tried out her new body, she found that she could dance just as well as ever. Indeed, now that she had the wings to balance herself, she could dance even more beautifully.

Meanwhile, her tribe were searching for her. They searched all over the plains and the hills and the desert. "Brolga!" they kept crying. "Brolga. Brolga. Where are you?"

Suddenly, a strange bird came running towards them, and started to dance. At first they didn't recognise her. They were about to chase her away, when they realised this strange bird was dancing one of their tribe's most sacred dances – and dancing it most beautifully. "It must be Brolga," they cried. "Brolga, come back to the camp with us, and we will look after you."

And from that day to this, you will find brolgas dancing round and round the places where Aboriginal Australians make their camp. And the Aboriginal people welcome them and feed them and never chase them away.

Brolgas

With its wide open spaces and so few predators, Australia is a paradise for birds, and it is home to two species of crane, the Sarus and the Brolga. Brolgas are slim, pale-grey birds about 1.3m (4.2 ft) tall. They live in the wetlands and plains of north and east Australia. Most of the time they go about in family groups of about a dozen; but in the mating season they come together to form flocks of up to a thousand.

They are famous for their courting ritual, when a male and a female leap and dance together, spreading their wings and singing. One of the Aboriginal ceremonial dances is based on this courting ritual. Brolgas, like swans, mate for life. Both mother and father share nest-building and incubating their eggs. Chicks stay with their parents until they are at least a year old.

These graceful birds are not a protected species, but their habitat is being reduced by the increasing use of plains and wetlands for agriculture.

Why the Platypus is such a special Creature

In the Dreamtime, the Creator made three different types of animal. First, he created Mammals. He told the Mammals they were to live on the land, and he gave them fur to keep them warm.

Next, he created Fish. He told the Fish they were to live in the water, and he gave them gills to help them breathe.

Then he created Birds. He told the Birds they were to live in the sky; he gave them wings to enable them to fly, and he gave the mother birds the ability to reproduce by laying eggs.

When the Creator had made these three different types of animal, he found there were a lot of bits and pieces left over. So he joined these bits and pieces together, and created Platypus.

Platypus are like no other creature on Earth. They have fur, like a mammal. They can swim underwater, like a fish. And the mother platypus lays eggs, like a bird.

At first the Mammals, the Fish and the Birds all lived happily together. But after a while they began to quarrel and fight. For each group thought it was the best and most important.

The Mammals held a meeting. Big Bagaray, the Kangaroo, thumped the ground with his tail. "We Mammals are the greatest!" he shouted. "We are special. Only we have fur."

"What about Platypus?" said his wife. "He has fur."

The Mammals thought about this. And they agreed to visit Platypus, and ask him if he would join them in their fight against the Fish and the Birds.

Platypus listened very carefully to all the Mammals had to say. Then he replied, "Thank you for asking me to be one of your family. I'll think about it."

A few days later, the Fish held a meeting. Goodoo, the big Murray Cod, leapt out of the water and came down with an almighty splash. "We Fish are the greatest!" he shouted. "We are special. Only we can swim under water."

"What about Platypus?" said his wife. "He spends most of his life under water.

The Fish thought about this. And they agreed to visit Platypus, and ask him if he would join them in their fight against the Mammals and the Birds.

Platypus listened very carefully to all the Fish had to say. Then he replied, "Thank you for asking me to be one of your family. I'll think about it."

Next, the Birds held a meeting. Bungil, the Eagle, spread and flapped his wings. The sound was like a tree falling. "We Birds are the greatest!" he shouted. "We are special. Only we can fly and lay eggs."

"What about Mrs Platypus?" said his wife. "She lays eggs."

The Birds thought about this. And they agreed to visit Platypus, and ask him if he would join them in their fight against the Mammals and the Fish.

Platypus listened very carefully to all the Birds had to say. Then he replied, "Thank you for asking me to be one of your family. I'll think about it."

Platypus thought and thought about what he should do. But no matter how hard he thought, he couldn't decide which group to join. After a while the animals got tired of waiting for him to make up his mind. They gathered outside his home on the bank of the billabong. The Mammals shouted, "Join us. We are the best!" The Fish shouted, "Join us. We are special!" The Birds shouted, "Join us. We are the best and special!"

At last, in the cool of the evening, Platypus came out. And all the animals fell silent.

"I've made up my mind," Platypus said. "I am part of each of you, and part of all of you. And that's how I want to stay. So thank you very much for asking me, but I've decided not to join any of you."

The animals didn't like this.

So Platypus went on, "Please let me explain. When the Creator first made us, he made each of us different. So each of us, in our own way, is special. But special doesn't mean better. None of us is better or worse than his neighbour. Only different. So we ought to respect each other's differences, and live together without fighting."

When the animals thought about this, they agreed that Platypus was very wise, and had made a good decision.

Now it so happened that, standing among the animals listening that evening to Platypus, was a hunter of the Pintubi tribe. This hunter was so impressed by what Platypus said, that he made his people promise never to harm such a wise creature.

Which is why no Aboriginal Australian will ever hunt and kill a Platypus – even if he is hungry.

Platypus

Only two mammals (creatures that suckle their young) lay eggs: the platypus and the echidna. Both live in Australia.

Platypus are less than 50 cms (18 ins) long. They are like no other creature on Earth. They have different-coloured layers of fur: brown, gold and grey. They also have scaly, beaver-like tails, big duck-like beaks, and webbed feet, with a poisonous spur on each hind foot. They spend much of their lives underwater and can swim as well as a fish.

The mother platypus lays eggs like a bird, but suckles her young like a mammal. No wonder the first platypus to be killed and sent back to Europe was thought to be a fake! Scientists didn't believe that such a strange creature could really exist.

Platypus are found in eastern Australia and Tasmania. They are shy, solitary creatures, coming together only to mate. They spend much of their time foraging for shrimps and insect larvae on the river bed. They hold their food in cheek-pouches, then bring it to the surface to eat. The females build huge riverbank burrows, sometimes 25m (over 27 yds) long, with a nesting chamber at the end. Here the mother platypus lays and guards her eggs – usually only one or two. When her eggs hatch, the babies suck milk from their mother's fur. These strange, endearing animals are classified as vulnerable and protected.

The Mountain Rose

Where the Blue Mountains rise up from the plains, there lived a beautiful girl whose name was Krubi. Krubi had many admirers. But she had thoughts for one man only: Bami, a young warrior to whom she was engaged.

Whenever Bami left their camp to go hunting, Krubi would climb into the mountains, and sit watching and waiting for him to return. She always took with her a bright-red kangaroo-skin cloak, to keep warm.

One day, a neighbouring tribe was caught hunting on land that belonged to Krubi's tribe. This was against the lore. Krubi's people were angry. And they told some of their warriors to drive the other tribe away. Among the warriors they sent out was Bami.

Before he left, Bami gave Krubi one of his spears. "Look after it for me," he said, "while I'm away. And when I come back, we will marry."

Krubi made her way to her favourite place in the mountains. She took with her Bami's long, slender spear and her bright red kangaroo-skin cloak. She watched the warriors as they headed into the plains. She watched them grow smaller and smaller and smaller, until they disappeared.

The hours passed. Soon it grew dark. But there was no sign of the warriors.

Some of Krubi's friends climbed up to where she was waiting. They said, "It is dangerous to stay by yourself at night in the mountains. The Spirit of Death will find you. Come back with us to our camp."

"I'm not afraid," said Krubi. "I'll wait for Bami until he returns."

She waited for him all that night, and all the next day.

And all the next day.

And the next.

She had almost given up hope when she saw, far, far away in the plains, some little black dots. The little black dots grew larger and larger. It was the warriors returning. There were not many of them.

Soon the warriors were close enough for Krubi to recognise them. Bami was not among them.

Krubi's friends again climbed up to her. They said, "It is no good waiting any longer. Bami must surely be dead. Come back with us to our camp, before Death finds you."

But Krubi wouldn't leave her place in the mountains. "Maybe," she said, "Bami isn't dead. Maybe he's only wounded. And if he comes back, he will need me."

But Bami didn't come back. And there came a time when Krubi knew that he must be in some other world.

Her heart was broken. She lost the will to live. She lay down, with Bami's spear beside her, and her bright-red kangaroo-skin coat wrapped round her, and stared into the plains. She went on staring into the plains until she died.

Not long afterwards, the weather grew colder, and Krubi's people left the Blue Mountains, and headed for a more sheltered place to make their camp. They did this every autumn. They were sad that Krubi was no longer with them. And the Elders said,

"Her love for Bami was something very special. We will always remember her." But even as the Elders spoke, they knew that memories don't really last forever, and that there would surely come a time when Krubi would be forgotten.

Some months later, when the weather grew warm again, Krubi's people came back to the Blue Mountains. They did this every spring. As they neared the mountains, they saw something that hadn't been there before – something small and red, high up in the mountains, waving about in the wind.

They climbed up to see what the strange, red thing was.

And there, in the place where Krubi had died, they found the most beautiful flower. Its stem was long, straight and slender, just like Bami's spear. Its flower was the shape of a heart. Its petals were the shape of falling tears, and it was the same bright red as Krubi's kangaroo-skin cloak.

It was Waratah, the first mountain rose.

"It is a gift from the Creator," the Elders said. "Now, whenever we look at Waratah, we will remember Krubi. Now we really *will* remember her for ever."

Waratah, the Mountain Rose

Australian flowers, like Australian animals, are unique – over 90% of the flowers that grow in Australia don't grow naturally anywhere else in the world. Most of Australia is very dry, and its plants have had to adapt to this. The continent's huge gum trees have tiny evergreen leaves in which they store water. The tiny spinifex grasses put down gigantic, 12-metre (40-ft) roots in search of moisture. Several plants, including the Waratah, are resistant to fire.

Aboriginal people prize the Waratah mainly because its seeds are edible. Europeans prize it mainly because of its beautiful, bright red flowers. It has become the official emblem of New South Wales. Today it is grown commercially, and you will find it in many gardens.

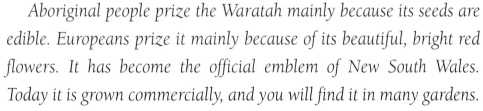
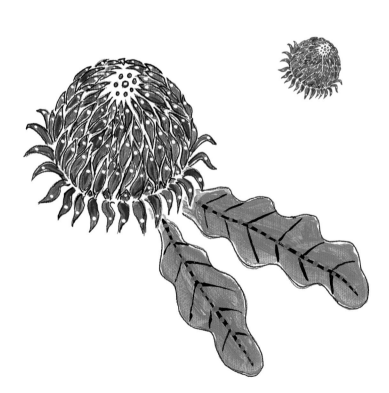

The Two Moths and the Flowers of the Mountain

Long ago, two moths lived in the plains at the foot of the mountains of the Great Divide. In those days, the mountains were bare and colourless. There were no flowers on them; just little patches of snow in winter.

Our two moths were as different as chalk from cheese.

Bogong, the man-moth, was a bit of a dull fellow. His wings were a drab grey and brown, and he never flew far from home.

Myee, his wife, was beautiful and adventurous. Her wings were wonderfully shaped and coloured. They were all reds and greens and blues and gold. They had almost as many colours in them as a rainbow.

Bogong and Myee were happy together – though Myee did sometimes wonder if, when she grew older and was no longer beautiful, her husband would still love her.

One day, she said to him, "Do you know what makes the top of the mountains go white?"

Bogong said he didn't know.

"I think I'll fly there," Myee said, "and find out."

Her husband didn't think much of this idea. "We are happy in the plains," he said. "Let us stay here. The mountains are another world, and dangerous. What goes on there doesn't concern us."

But Myee wouldn't be put off. And one autumn morning, she set out to fly to the mountains.

The mountains looked near. But Myee's wings were small, and though she flew as fast as she could, and never stopped for a rest,

it took her a long, long time to reach the mountains. By the time she got there, she was very tired. And it was getting dark and cold.

Looking up, Myee could see that the mountains above her were white. "If I fly just a little higher," she said to herself, "I'll be able to see what the white stuff is."

Suddenly it started to snow.

For Myee, the snowflakes were a disaster. They settled on and stuck to her wings. Her wings beat slower and slower. And slower and slower. And slower still – until there came a time when they couldn't beat at all. And, like a plane without its engines, poor Myee spiralled round and round and down and down, until she crashed into the side of the mountain.

Bruised and frightened, she crawled into a crevice between the rocks.

The snow fell and fell and fell. It kept on falling. After a while the top layer of snow turned to ice. Myee was trapped, sealed up like a fly in amber. She shut her eyes, and slept.

She slept all winter.

It was the warmth of the spring sun that woke her. Opening her eyes, she saw that the snow and ice had disappeared. She crawled out from among the rocks.

She spread her wings. And, to her surprise, saw they were a dull grey. Their beautiful colours had gone.

She looked down the mountainside. And, to her amazement, she saw that it was covered by a carpet of the most beautiful flowers.

The flowers were wonderfully shaped and coloured. They were all reds and greens and blues and gold. They had almost as many colours in them as a rainbow.

The melting snow had washed the colours out of Myee's wings, and turned them into the most lovely flowers.

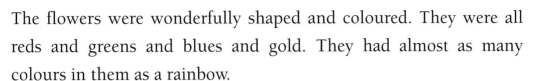

Myee flew back to the plains.

She was afraid that now she was no longer beautiful, her husband might not want her back. But she need not have worried. Bogong had spent all winter searching for her. He was overjoyed to see her. Together they danced over the plains.

"I fear I am no longer beautiful," Myee said.

"You have passed on your beauty to the flowers of the mountains," her husband said. "Now, each spring, with the coming of the flowers, your beauty will be born again. Now you don't have to worry about it fading. Now you can be sure it will last for ever."

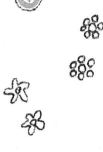

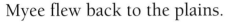

Bogong Moths and Mountain and Desert Flowers

Bogong moths are found in great numbers all over non-tropical Australia. They are a pale, mottled brown, and have a wing-span of only 4 or 5 cms (1.5 ins). Each year they migrate in huge swarms between the hot plains and the cooler coast. They are attracted to lights; and in cities such as Canberra, the Bogong swarms can cause great inconvenience to local people by blocking air-conditioning ducts and setting off alarms. Nomadic Aboriginal Australians used to eat the swarming moths, which have a high protein content, and taste a bit like walnut.

The flowers of Australia's mountains and deserts can be spectacular, but because it is often so dry, they are usually short-lived. Some annuals (plants which live only one year) have drought-resistant seeds; the seeds of the Sturt's desert pea can lie dormant for ten years. Some perennials (plants which live several years) shed all their flowers, leaves and stems when it is dry, and can't be seen above ground; they store what little moisture there is in big underground roots.

How the Crocodile got its Scales

In the Dreamtime, a tribe called the Gunivugi lived beside a beautiful, slow-flowing river. There were no dangerous animals in the river, and the Gunivugi often went swimming.

One of the tribe's most skilful hunters was a tall, handsome young man whose name was Pukawah. Few could equal Pukawah with the spear, the fishing-net or the boomerang. But he was vain and foolish. And he fell in love with a married woman.

This was against the lore.

The elders of the tribe told Pukawah that he was behaving badly, but he laughed at them and went on seeing the woman.

The elders were uncertain what to do. Some of them thought that Pukawah ought to be punished. Some thought that he ought to be forgiven. They decided to ask the Great Spirit for advice.

And the Great Spirit said. "Give Pukawah one last chance. But tell him that if he doesn't mend his ways, he will be punished, and punished severely."

The elders did as the Great Spirit suggested.

But a few days later Pukawah and the woman were seen together beside the river.

The tribe lost patience. The woman's husband and relatives and a great crowd of warriors took their spears and made their way to the river.

Pukawah saw them coming and tried to run away; but they cornered him. They flung their spears at him. Again and again and again. The spears sank deep into Pukawah's back. He gave a great cry,

and toppled into the river. The water closed over his head and he disappeared.

The Gunivugi felt sure that Pukawah was dead, and that they had seen the last of him.

But they were wrong.

Some weeks later, a monstrous creature came crawling out of the river. Its back was covered with hard bony scales. These were the heads of the spears that had sunk into Pukawah's back – the shafts had rotted away in the water. The creature started to crawl towards the place where the Gunivugi were camped. But they saw it coming, and drove it back into the river.

Then Pukawah – for that is who the creature was – heard the voice of the Great Spirit. "Because you broke the lore, you are condemned to live for ever in the water. And because you broke the lore, your children and the children of the Gunivugi will never have fun and play together."

So it came about that whenever the Gunivugi went down to the river to bathe, a crocodile would rush at them and attack them. And whenever a crocodile left the river and crawled on to the land, the Gunivugi would rush at it and attack it.

As it was in the Dreamtime, so it is today – and perhaps will be for ever.

Crocodiles

Crocodiles are survivors from the age of the dinosaurs. They have altered little in the last 65 million years. They live in tropical rivers, lakes, swamps and estuaries. Two types of crocodile live in the hot and humid northern part of Australia. The Johnson, a freshwater crocodile, can grow to be about 2.7m (9 ft) long. The Estuarine or estuary-dweller, a saltwater crocodile, can grow as long as 6m (20 ft) and weighs nearly 1 tonne (1.10 tons).

Estuarines are dangerous flesh-eaters. They can kill animals as big as a buffalo, and it is thought that each year more people in the world are killed by crocodiles than by any other predatory animal.

In spite of their fierceness, crocodile mothers are tender and loving. A mother lays 50-80 eggs in a nest on the riverbank. She guards them until they hatch. As soon as her babies are born, she carries them very gently in her mouth to the edge of the river, where they start feeding on shrimps and insects. Less than half of her babies will survive their first year.

The Lizard-Man and the Creation of Uluru

Alinga, the Lizard-Man, was one of the beings of the Dreamtime – the time when Aboriginal people believe the world was created. He was a mighty warrior. His favourite weapon was the boomerang. He could throw a boomerang so far, it sometimes took days to return.

One day, Alinga decided to make a special boomerang, throw it as far as he could, and see how long it took to come back.

He gathered together the branches of eucalypt trees, and laid them out in a great half circle. Then, with the sinews of kangaroos' tails, he tied the branches together. He collected the seeds of spinifex grass. Then he made fire, and melted the seeds until they turned into a sort of sticky glue. With this glue he sealed up the cracks and crevices in the boomerang he was creating. Finally, he polished it with the wax of wild bees.

At last the great boomerang was ready. Alinga flexed his muscles. He drew back his arm, and with all his strength flung the boomerang high into the sky. With a great *whrrrrrrr*, like a flight of cockatoos, it disappeared over the mountains.

Alinga waited for it to return. He waited patiently, hour after hour. The hours turned into days. The days turned into weeks. The weeks turned into months. The months turned into years. And still there was no sign of the boomerang.

Alinga decided to go and look for it.

He climbed the mountains, and set out across the desert. Whenever he met anyone he asked them if they had seen his boomerang. But no-one had.

One day, he met a family who didn't know what a boomerang was. He showed them how to make one, and how to throw it. Then he set off once again on his journey.

He journeyed across great deserts, over high mountains, and through dark rainforests. He journeyed on and on and on, year after year after year. But he couldn't find his boomerang.

He had many adventures.

Sometimes at night, when he felt cold, he made a camp fire. Today, at these places, you will find coal.

More than once, as he passed by a billabong, he was attacked by evil bunyips. They fought. And today, at these places, you will find the bodies of the bunyips turned into great boulders lying on the beds of the billabongs.

More than once, as he crossed the plains, he was attacked by giant wild dingoes. They fought. And today, at these places, you will find the bodies of the dingoes turned into the huge rock formations that lie scattered across the outback.

He was not far from Kata Tjuta (the great rocks known sometimes as the Olgas) when he saw in the distance a huge red dome, rising out of the desert. It was shaped like an enormous boomerang.

As he neared it, Alinga saw it really *was* a boomerang: his special boomerang, which had crashed into the desert, and, over the years, had been covered with layer after layer of dust and sand, until it turned into a huge, red block of rock.

Alinga was delighted to see his boomerang again. He took hold of it and tried to lift it. But it was too heavy. For days, he struggled to raise it. Where his fingers dug into the rock, gulleys and caves were formed – you can see them to this day. But the boomerang

was embedded too deep. Not even the mighty Lizard-Man could move it.

Alinga didn't want to be parted from his boomerang, so he settled down to live beside it. It is said that he performed many great feats while living beside his boomerang in the desert.

It is also said that the great numbers of lizards now living in the caves at the foot of the big red rock known as Uluru are the spiritual descendants of Alinga the Lizard-Man.

Uluru

Uluru, which used to be known as Ayers Rock, is one of the wonders of the natural world: a huge outcrop of rock, 9.4 km (six miles) in circumference, rising almost vertically out of the desert to a height of over a thousand feet. There are two explanations as to how it was formed.

According to scientists, Uluru is the top of a buried hill. They say that about 130 million years ago, the sea flooded into central Australia, turning Uluru into an island, and that the waves pounding the shore of the island formed great caves. Then the sea ebbed away, leaving Uluru surrounded by sand.

According to some Aboriginal Australians, Uluru was created by the Lizard-Man. But to other Aboriginal people its rocks are the actual bones of their ancestral heroes of the Dreamtime – the legendary beginning of the world. Some of its caves are covered with the most beautiful Aboriginal rock paintings, tens of thousands of years old; they are now being retouched to revive their symbolic powers.

In 1986 the Australian Government returned the ownership of Uluru to the Aboriginal people. The rock is now under the joint control of the Aboriginal people and the Australian National Parks and Wildlife Services, who safeguard it as a shrine and a tourist attraction. Aboriginal Australians would be grateful if visitors didn't climb Uluru, since for them it is a sacred place.

The Butterflies and the Mystery of Death

In the Dreamtime, the creatures on Earth all lived happily together. And they didn't know what death was. Every spring, they would gather beside the Murray River. The old ones would sit and talk, while the young ones splashed about in the river, or played hide and seek in the trees.

One day, all of a sudden, Gingee the cockatoo fell off a high branch in one of the gum trees and broke his neck. He lay on the ground, very still. The animals gathered round him and tried to wake him. But they couldn't. They prodded him with a stick, but he didn't feel anything. They opened his eyes, but he couldn't see.

The animals were puzzled. They decided to call a meeting to discuss what could have happened to Gingee.

First, they asked Youreil the owl to give his explanation. Because Youreil had big round eyes that could see just about everything, he was thought to be very wise. But Youreil had to admit he had no idea what had happened.

Then Mullian the eaglehawk jumped up. He took a stone, and threw it into the river. The stone hit the water, and disappeared. "That is what happened to the cockatoo," Mullian said. "As far as we are concerned, he has disappeared. It is as though he had never been."

The animals were not too happy with this explanation.

Then Whan the crow jumped up. He took a piece of wood, and threw it into the river. The piece of wood disappeared for a moment, then rose to the surface and was carried away downstream.

"That is what happened to the cockatoo," Whan said. "As far as we are concerned, he has disappeared. But he will reappear in another place."

The animals thought about this. And they agreed to put Whan's theory to the test. Several animals said they would make themselves, like Gingee the cockatoo, unable to feel, see, hear or smell. Then they would see if, after a while, they reappeared in a different place. So the goannas, the possums, the wombats, the frogs and the snakes crawled into holes in the ground, sealed themselves up so they couldn't feel, see, hear or smell, and went to sleep. They hibernated. Then after several months, they woke and came crawling out of their holes.

But they found they were still in the same place. Nothing had changed. Except that they were all a lot thinner. And very hungry.

The animals agreed that this couldn't be what had happened to Gingee.

Then a whole lot of insects jumped up. "We know what happened to the cockatoo!" they shouted.

At first, the animals took no notice, for the insects were thought to be small and a bit silly. But the beetles, the water-bugs and caterpillars kept shouting, "We know! We know! We know!" And at last Youreil said, "All right. What's your explanation?"

The insects said they wouldn't *tell* the other animals what had happened to Gingee – they would *show* them. They said they would go to sleep. And when they woke, it would be obvious to everyone what had happened to the cockatoo.

So the water-bugs wrapped themselves in tea-tree bark, and floated away in the billabong. And the caterpillars nestled into the leaves of the gum trees. And they slept. And slept. And slept. All winter.

When it was spring, the wattle bushes turned the most beautiful yellow, and the mountain rose the most beautiful red. But there was no sign of the insects.

The animals decided to hold another meeting. They were wondering what on Earth could have happened to the water-bugs and the caterpillars, when Mullian the eaglehawk shouted, "Look!"

Up the valley came what appeared to be a moving rainbow: a mass of red and yellow, purple and green, orange and blue. The rainbow came dancing towards them. As it got nearer, the animals heard the rustle of tens of thousands of wings. The butterflies – for that is who they were – flew round and round the animals. "Don't you recognise us?" they cried. "We are the water-bugs and the caterpillars!"

The butterflies danced in the warmth of the sun. They settled now on the wattle bushes, now on the waratah. Then, in a great rainbow-coloured cloud, they flew high into the mountains.

When they had disappeared, Youreil said to the animals, "Now we know what happened to Gingee. To us, he may have disappeared, but he will reappear later in another form. Now, at last, we understand death."

Hibernation and Metamorphosis

Many animals hibernate, including goannas, possums, wombats, frogs, snakes and bats. When conditions are difficult and food is scarce, they crawl into a safe hiding-place. Once there, they don't sleep and they don't eat. Everything closes down: their movement, their heartbeat, their breathing – a hibernating bat needs to take a breath only once every two hours. At the end of their hibernation, these creatures emerge almost unchanged.

Even more Australian creatures, such as butterflies, go through metamorphosis – their bodies change from one form to another. Australia has over 400 different species of butterfly. They lay their eggs among flowers, grasses or leaves. Each egg turns into a caterpillar. Each caterpillar, after a while, builds a cocoon, and inside this cocoon its body breaks down and is rearranged – rearranged into a butterfly. The butterfly then emerges from its cocoon and flies away.

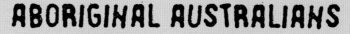

ABORIGINAL AUSTRALIANS

The Aboriginal people were the first Australians. They are thought to have migrated from Indonesia to Australia during the last Ice Age, over 60,000 years ago. Sea levels were lower then, and a landbridge connected Australia to New Guinea. When the Ice Age ended and sea levels rose again, Aboriginal Australians found themselves cut off from the rest of the world. They were therefore able to develop, in isolation, a unique way of life – the oldest continuing culture on Earth.

Early European settlers thought the Aboriginal people primitive; but in fact they lived in complex, well-structured social groups and had a rich cultural tradition and profound spiritual beliefs. Their belief systems were bound spiritually to the Earth. "An Aborigine's altars are his waterholes, hills and rocks", writes the anthropologist Colin Simpson. "He is identified with and bound to his tribal land."

European settlers soon drove Aboriginal people off their tribal lands. Those who resisted were killed. In Tasmania the entire Aboriginal population was wiped out. Only in recent years have efforts been made to return some of their land, thus enabling Aboriginal Australians to regain their faith, their culture and their dignity.

Glossary

Barramundi – fish of the grouper family found in the rivers and coastal waters of North Australia. They average about 60 cm (2 ft) in length and 2.7 kg(6 lb) in weight. They have a white body covered in small black dots, and are very good to eat.

Billabong – a waterhole, pond, or any place where a fair amount of water collects and lies undisturbed.

Babook – small, brown Australian owl that roosts in trees during the day, and hunts at night. It has a high-pitched "*book-book*" call.

Boomerang – a flat, curved, wooden, hand-thrown weapon, originally used by Aboriginal people for hunting, nowadays sometimes used for recreation. Boomerangs are designed so that they have a curved flight-path, and return towards the person who threw them.

Bunyip – mythical, big, hairy, scary monster that lives in waterholes and shallow rivers, and eats small animals and unwary children.

Cassowary – a large, flightless bird, about 1.5m (5 ft) in height and 45 kg (100 lb) in weight. It lives in the tropical forests of North Queensland.

Cockatoo – a species of parrot-like birds found all over Australia. There are about 18 different species, several of which are popular as pets. They are gregarious and often gather in large, noisy flocks.

Dingo – wild dog believed to be descended from the domestic dogs brought to Australia by Aboriginal people tens of thousands of years ago. Its colour ranges from dun to russet; it has a bushy tail, and never barks. In many parts of Australia it is regarded as a pest.

Dreamtime – the time when Aboriginal Australians believe the Earth was shaped and populated. Dreamtime legends tell how giants and animals sprang from the Earth and created its physical features such as mountains and billabongs.

Emu – a big, flightless bird with long legs and tiny wings, averaging 1.8m (6 ft) in height and a little over 45 kg (100 lb) in weight. The father bird incubates his partner's eggs and cares for their chicks.

Galah – a type of cockatoo (see page 57) common all over Australia.

Goanna – a large lizard found throughout rural Australia. Averaging about 0.9m (3 ft) in length, they have long flexible tails which they use both as a weapon and as a prop when standing on their back legs. They are fierce predators, feeding on almost any bird, mammal or reptile smaller than themselves.

Gum tree – the common name for Australia's distinctive and most successful tree, the eucalyptus. Because they have to exist in many different habitats – dry deserts, snow-covered mountains and humid rainforests – they have diversified into many different species, ranging from the huge 91-m (300-ft) mountain ash to the tiny 0.9-m (3-ft) desert mallee. Most have drooping grey-green, evergreen, resinous leaves. Some have shiny bark to reflect the heat. Some are resistant to fire.

Kookaburra – the largest of the kingfishers, famous for its raucous, laugh-like call. Kookaburras live in small family groups, and sometimes become so tame they can be fed by hand.

Marsupial – a mammal which gives birth to and carries its young in an external pouch (*marsupion* comes from the Greek word meaning 'a little purse or bag'). Its babies are born after a very short gestation, sometimes only a few days, and are very small, sometimes no more than 2.5cm (1 in) long. Most marsupials, such as kangaroos, live in Australia; but some, such as the possum, are also found in America.

Possum – a furry, nocturnal animal with a long tail, about the size of a domestic cat. Some possums live in trees and make a loud noise at nighttime when they argue among themselves. (Some American possums, when threatened, pretend to be dead, lying for up to six hours without moving – hence the phrase 'playing possum'.)

Spinifex – a short, tough, spiny grass found in Australia's deserts and arid plains. It can exist in sand, drought and unbelievably harsh conditions, putting down roots 9m (30 feet) long in search of water.

Wattle bush – a species of Acacia with beautiful yellow flowers which has become the emblem of Australia.

Wombat – a powerfully-built, badger-like marsupial about 1m (3 ft) in length and 30 kg (70lb) in weight. Wombats graze by night on grasses and roots. They are great burrowers, and their tunnels are sometimes over 180m (600 ft) long.

Aboriginal symbols and their meanings

Aboriginal art is full of symbols.

Each symbol has a meaning.

How many of the symbols shown here

can you find in this book?

small waterhole

waterhole

dry or bad waterhole

tree

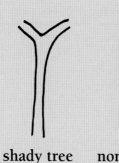

shady tree   non-shady tree

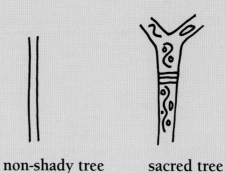

sacred tree

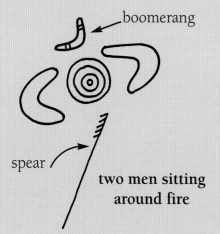

boomerang

spear

two men sitting around fire

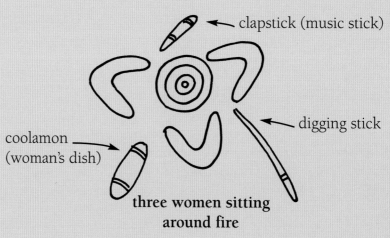

clapstick (music stick)

coolamon (woman's dish)

digging stick

three women sitting around fire

sun

moon and stars

mountains and hills

60

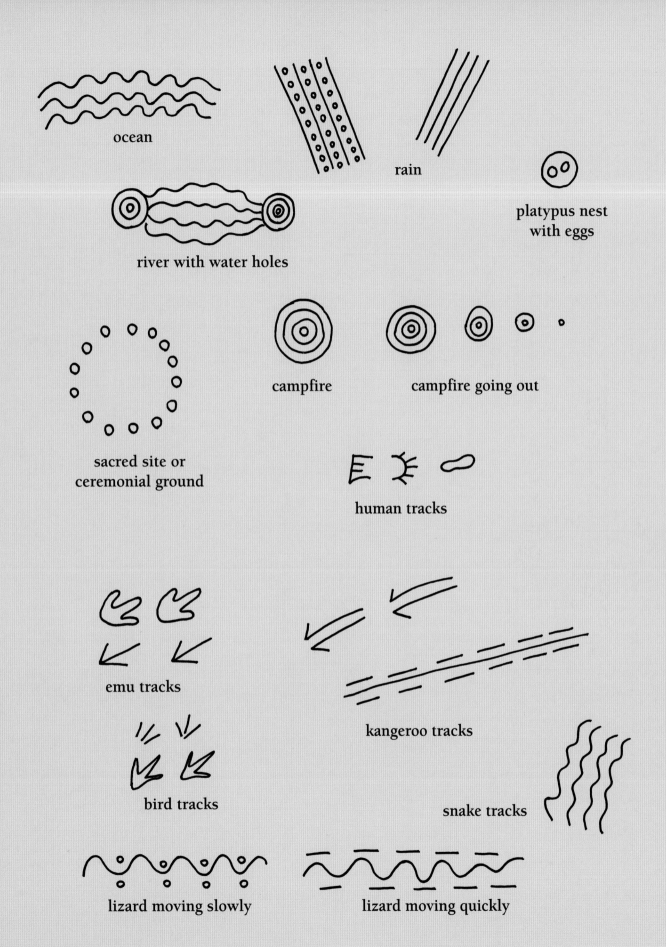

ocean

rain

platypus nest
with eggs

river with water holes

sacred site or
ceremonial ground

campfire

campfire going out

human tracks

emu tracks

kangeroo tracks

bird tracks

snake tracks

lizard moving slowly

lizard moving quickly

61